I LOST MY BEAR

JULES FEIFFER

MORROW JUNIOR BOOKS
NEW YORK

Watercolor and ink were used for the full-color illustrations.
The text type is hand-lettered.
Copyright © 1998 by Jules Feiffer

Published by Morrow Junior Books
a division of William Morrow and Company, Inc.
1350 Avenue of the Americas, New York, NY 10019
www.williammorrow.com

Printed in the United States of America.

10 9 8 7 6 5 4 3

Library of Congress Cataloging-in-Publication Data
Feiffer, Jules.
I lost my bear/Jules Feiffer.
p. cm.
Summary: When she cannot find her
favorite stuffed toy, a young girl asks her
mother, father, and older sister for help.
ISBN 0-688-15147-7 (trade)—ISBN 0-688-15148-5 (library)
[1. Lost and found possessions—Fiction. 2. Family life—Fiction.]
I. Title. PZ7.F33345Iaf 1998 97-34475 CIP AC

For Charlotte

I KNOW IT'S
SOMEWHERE . . .

UH-OH...

I can't find my bear.

I asked my mother.

I tried to think like a detective and remember where I was playing with it last.

I think I was playing with it last under the bed.

But I don't see it.

Maybe I was playing with it last in the bookcase.

Hmm. I don't see it.

Was I playing with it last in the living room?

It's not on the couch.

Or behind the curtains. It's not under the chairs.

So . . .

I asked my sister.

And she said:

Nobody will help me find my bear.

So I cried.

And nobody stopped me.

So I stopped myself.

But I know it's gone

forever.

My sister said:

But which stuffed animal?

If I throw one of my favorites,
what if I lose that one too?

So I better throw a stuffed animal
I don't care about.

But if I pick one I don't care about,
it will know.

And it won't want to find my lost bear.

My bunny rabbit is my second favorite stuffed animal after my bear.

I can't do it!

I go to my sister.

I have the best sister in the world!

I closed my eyes.

And I threw it!

And it found my lost barrette.

Then it found my lost kitten.

But she wasn't really lost, she was hiding.

Then it found my lost Magic Markers.

So I drew a picture of my lost bear.

Then ...

my one last extra-special-I-really-mean-it-this-time throw.

It found my lost purse.

And inside my purse was a bunch of other things I lost.

So I played with them.

Until bedtime ...

When my mother said:

OH, MY GOSH! I forgot all about my bear!

I cried.

Because I was ashamed I forgot about my bear.

Aren't I the best detective?

8-15

E   Feiffer, Jules
          I lost my bear.